Charlie Meets
Hobart the Wizard

Special thanks to family and friends
for their support and encouragement.

To the Hampstead Library
and all of its readers
Enjoy. Best wishes
Charles Elias

‹·—————————————❧—————————————·›

ISBN: 978-0-9996188-7-5
Printed in the United States of America.

This book can be purchased on
Amazon.com.

Author resides in Sandown, NH

Charlie Meets Hobart the Wizard

by
Charles
Elias

Illustrations by
Mike Motz

Long ago in a faraway land lived an inquisitive boy named Charlie…

Charlie is a funny boy who is twelve years old. He sits in his kitchen chair, balancing a spoon on his nose. His dad is constantly telling him that he needs to find a job.

"Stop messing around, Charlie," says Charlie's dad. "Hanging around the house isn't going to help us survive the long winter months." Charlie's dad, Joe, works as a logger down the road and had injured his back while moving logs. His work slows down during the winter months, which doesn't help the family's living situation. Charlie lives with his parents and two brothers. Charlie knows he must start looking for a part time job in order to help his family.

"Why don't you try working with Peter the Blacksmith? He is a good friend," says Joe. Peter is a strong but tolerant man that could put up with Charlie's nonsense. Charlie just wants to have fun.

Early the next morning, Charlie has a delicious pancake breakfast. After saddling up, Charlie heads down the road with his horse, Fred. After traveling through the forest, he takes a dirt road towards the town of Loretta.

"Fred, keep the pace," says Charlie. Fred is an old horse and has sore legs after walking over the rocks on the dirt road. "Fred, are you having a tough time walking?"

Fred looks tired, but he perks up when he notices water troughs in front of the stores. Loretta is an old town that has all of the shops needed for its people. The Blacksmith Shop is on the right side of the road where Peter the Blacksmith is making shoes for a horse.

"Hello, Mr. Blacksmith. I am Joe's son, looking for work," says Charlie.

"Oh yes, Joe's son," remarks Peter. "I am a bit swamped today and could use your help. I will give you one shilling for the day." As Peter stands next to Fred, he notices the horse's knees are worn and mentions it to Charlie.

"Fred did have a tough time walking today," replies Charlie.

"Fred can rest in my horse stable while you work tomorrow," replies Peter.

When Charlie arrives the next day, he helps Peter hammer out metal horse shoes. "Boy, this is hard work," says Charlie. Charlie continues working throughout that day, next to the hot fire pit.

"We have to heat up the metal first, then hammer the metal into the shape of horse shoes," says Peter.

Charlie works hard throughout the day, wishing he can go out to play. When he finishes his last shoe, he gets one shilling, as Peter had promised. Charlie was happy to learn a new skill. He uses the shilling at the General Store to buy one bushel of potatoes for his family.

Charlie places the potatoes on the horse's back in a leather sack and makes it home late in the evening. Mom and Dad thanked Charlie for the potatoes that he has brought home. "A job well done!" says Charlie's dad.

"How was work today?" asks his mom.

"Today went fine, but I'll tell you it was hard work," replies Charlie. "Peter was a nice guy but made sure the work got done."

"You have to get your work done if you want to get paid," replies Joe. "Did you hear about a Wizard that lives in a cave in Loretta?"

"I did hear talk in town about him, but most people thought it was just hearsay," replies Charlie. "It would be nice to be able to use some magic, then we could have all the food we need."

"Dreaming again, Charlie," replies Charlie's dad.

Stew was the boy's favorite meal. Dad had wrapped pieces of beef in paper in the barn but the pieces of beef had spoiled and Joe was upset. "I can find another day job to help out," says Charlie.

"Thank you, Charlie. That would be helpful while my back heals," Dad replies. "Let's eat."

The hot stew smells delicious. The family sits down and enjoys their dinner.

Early the next morning, Charlie asks his dad about finding work.

His dad replies, "Charlie, my friend Bob needs help at his carpentry shop. I will let him know you will be there tomorrow."

Charlie's dad's back is feeling stronger, and he will be returning to work in a few days.

Later that morning, Charlie heads out to Loretta after feeding Fred. After traveling for a while, Charlie's horse is thirsty. Charlie guides Fred over to the side of the creek for a drink of water. Charlie notices the townspeople purchasing goods and having repairs done in town. The next stop down the road was the Carpentry Shop, where Joe's friend Bob is busy at work repairing rocking chairs.

"Sir, would you be in need of a helper?" asks Charlie.

"Yes," replies Bob. "Today, I can use the help gluing my rocking chairs. I could pay you a shilling for your help today and for an additional day of work, I will pay you two shillings." Bob shows Charlie how to make some of the repairs by gluing the legs on the bottom of the chairs.

Charlie notices a woman that had been complaining about getting her rocking chair repaired. She cries out, "Mr. Bob, when will my chair be repaired?"

"Your chair will be repaired soon, Miss Susan. I have a helper today," replies Bob.

While Charlie works, he notices a dog run by and a boy throwing a ball to his dog. Charlie wishes he could be playing outside, but he knows how the money will help his family. The following day, he glues and repairs the last remaining chairs and gets paid two shillings as Bob had promised.

That evening, Charlie rides down the road to buy some rice at the General Store. The storekeeper's name is Miss Laura. She had just sold some flour to one of her customers. Charlie waits, then gets a large burlap bag of rice from her. Charlie thanks her, and then before saddling up, he picks up a package of beef at the Butcher Shop.

On his way home, he notices a chubby little mouse running across the bridge with an orange shirt a pair of red pants and a straw hat. "Hey, little mouse, where are you going?" shouts Charlie.

"I am going to see Hobart the Wizard."

"I would love to meet the Wizard," replies Charlie.

"Meet me here tomorrow and I will show you the cave where he practices his Wizardry," replies the little mouse. "Just look for me on this road and call my name, Ziggy, two times and I will appear." Suddenly the mouse vanishes.

How magical! Charlie thinks. Charlie cannot wait to meet Hobart the Wizard.

Later in the evening, Charlie returns home with the rice and beef he had purchased in town. Charlie's parents greet him and thank him for working for the much needed food. With excitement, Charlie asks his father if he can meet with Hobart the Wizard.

Dad said that will be okay, but to be careful! After a long ride, Charlie is glad to see his brothers, and as soon he puts his head down on his pillow, he falls fast asleep.

The next day, Charlie awakes with a burst of energy and cannot wait to visit Hobart the Wizard.

Charlie gets dressed then rides with Fred to look for Ziggy the mouse. Charlie calls out the mouse's name on the bridge, where he had seen him the day before. "Ziggy, Ziggy," calls Charlie.

Suddenly, Ziggy the mouse appears, sitting on the side of the bridge.

"Here I am!" shouts out Ziggy. "I know I promised you a trip to the Wizard's cave. Hobart would like to show you his magic today."

Ziggy jumps up onto Fred's back with Charlie. Charlie places the little mouse onto his leather bag behind Charlie's saddle. By evening, after a long weary ride, they finally approach the cave. Fred is exhausted and lies down to rest by a large rock. Charlie is astonished to see Hobart the Wizard levitating a leaf into the air.

Suddenly a little fairy with two wings on her back appears outside the cave, wearing a yellow dress.

"Welcome! My name is Lindsay. Hobart is expecting you today," says the fairy. "Today he is practicing his magic."

As Charlie follows the fairy into the cave, he hears the Wizard's voice echo. "What is your name, young man?" Hobart asks.

"My name is Charlie," replies Charlie.

"If you want to practice magic with me, you need to offer me something useful," says Hobart. "Then I will let you choose two spells."

"Okay, Mr. Wizard!" replies Charlie. "I have learned how to make iron shoes for horses, taught by Peter the Blacksmith and how to repair rocking chairs, from Bob the carpenter."

"With all of these skillful jobs," says Hobart the Wizard, "I can use your talents to make some new iron shoes for my horse, Sam, and repair my favorite wooden rocking chair."

The Wizard gives Charlie the metal pieces he needs to make four horse shoes and the wood and glue he needs to repair the rocking chair. Charlie works feverishly until the horse shoes were made and chair was repaired. Charlie was finished before long and Hobart thanks Charlie for his repairs. "Now, I will teach you two spells that I promised you" replied Hobart.

"First I would like to learn how to levitate objects, so I can help my dad," says Charlie. "After Dad cuts down trees, I can load the trees into his wagon. My second spell would be learning a way to help my old horse Fred live a happier life without pain. Since he is an old horse, he can use some youthful energy."

"I can teach you how to perform levitating," says Hobart. "But I have no spell to keep your horse alive forever." I can teach you a spell so you can understand your horse's language.

"Levitating a small rock will be a start. Remember, Charlie, you will use this stick as a magic wand from now on," says Hobart. Charlie holds the stick that the Wizard gave him. Then Hobart places one hand below and one hand above the top of Charlie's hands. The most extraordinary thing happens. A warm glow wraps around Charlie's hands. When he tries to levitate the rock, it just falls to the ground. But on his second try, the rock vibrates and floats above the ground. Charlie is amazed!

"Great job levitating the rock!" says Hobart. "Rest tonight, and tomorrow I will teach you a new spell so you can speak to your horse."

Charlie cannot wait to help Fred. He soon falls asleep on the cave floor with a blanket that Hobart had given him. Ziggy sleeps on a rock shelf in the cave with his red blanket.

Charlie wakes up the next morning and finds his friend Ziggy standing on a rock by his side.

Ziggy asks, "Will you learn a spell today?"

"Yes, Ziggy," replies Charlie.

Then Hobart appears and asks, "Are you ready to learn your new spell today?"

"Yes, I am ready to learn," Charlie replies.

"Go out of the cave and bring in Fred," Hobart says.

"Okay," replies Charlie.

When the horse entered the cave, Hobart said to Charlie, "Repeat after me three times: lazarru, lazarru, lazarru while holding your wand and pointing it to Fred's nose."

Charlie repeats the spell, "Lazarru, lazarru, lazarru," holding his wand to Fred's nose.

Suddenly, Fred rears up and says to Charlie in a deep voice, "Please don't touch my nose."

Charlie realizes that Fred is talking to him and that the spell has worked! He can communicate with his horse! "Fred what bothers you?" asks Charlie.

Fred replies, "My legs hurt and are worn out. Tell the Wizard to make a magical lotion and rub it on my legs. This magic lotion will sooth my aching legs from the soreness."

Charlie asks the Wizard to make the magic lotion for Fred. The Wizard mixed different herbs together and makes his lotion. Soon after Charlie applied the lotion on Fred's legs, the pain subsided. Charlie thanks the Wizard for helping Fred and for teaching him how to levitate objects.

As Charlie rides off, Hobart says, "Maybe I will see you again someday."

When Charlie turns around, the Wizard is waving good-bye and then disappears into a mist.

On the way home, Fred says, "My legs feel great."

"Oh, I am glad you feel renewed," says Charlie.

Charlie's dad is happy that he has a much stronger horse and a son who can levitate objects. His dad needs help with his wagon; the wooden wheel has fallen off. "No work tomorrow if I can't get this wagon fixed," says Joe.

Charlie points his magic wand at the wheel and it rises off the ground onto the wagon. "Great job!" remarked Joe. Charlie's dad is happy that his son has learned magic from Hobart and that Charlie can help with the family chores.

CPSIA information can be obtained at www.ICGtesting.com
Printed in the USA
BVIW12n1817250318
511485BV00001B/3